The Sun and the Wind

An Aesop Fable Retold by Cornelia Lehn
Illustrated by Robert W. Regier

Faith and Life Press
Newton, Kansas

Library of Congress Number 32-0000
International Standard Book Number 0-87303-072-9
Printed in the United States of America
Copyright © 1983 by Faith and Life Press
718 Main Street, Newton, Kansas 67114

Illustrated by Robert W. Regier
Printed by Mennonite Press, Inc.

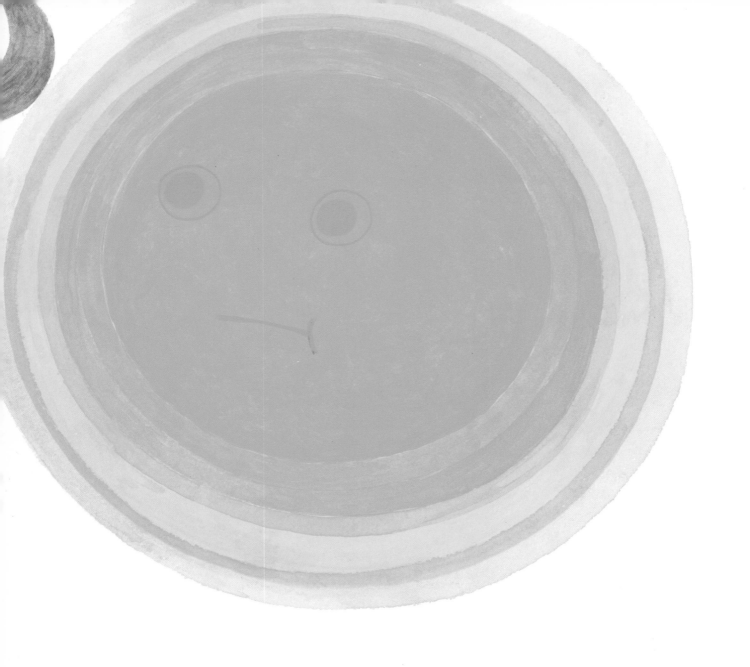

The sun and the wind were having an argument.

"Nothing is stronger than force," howled the wind.
"I can make people do anything I want them to
if I blow hard enough!"
"Love is much stronger than force," smiled the sun.
"When I shine warmly, people want to cooperate."

"Non-s-s-sens-s-s-e!" hissed the wind.

"Want to bet?" winked the sun.

"Sure — sure — sure!
I'll show you I'm right," whistled the wind.

"All right," said the sun.
"See that man down there?"

"Yes," whirled the wind. "What about him?"

"He is wearing a coat.
I bet I can persuade him to take it off
but you can't make him do it," grinned the sun.

"Ho, ho, ho," roared the wind.
"I'll show you! I'll show you!"

"Very well," said the sun. "Go ahead!"

The wind blew hard.
The man buttoned one of the buttons on his coat.
The wind blew harder.
The man buttoned another button on his coat.

The wind blew harder and harder.
The man buttoned the third button on his coat.

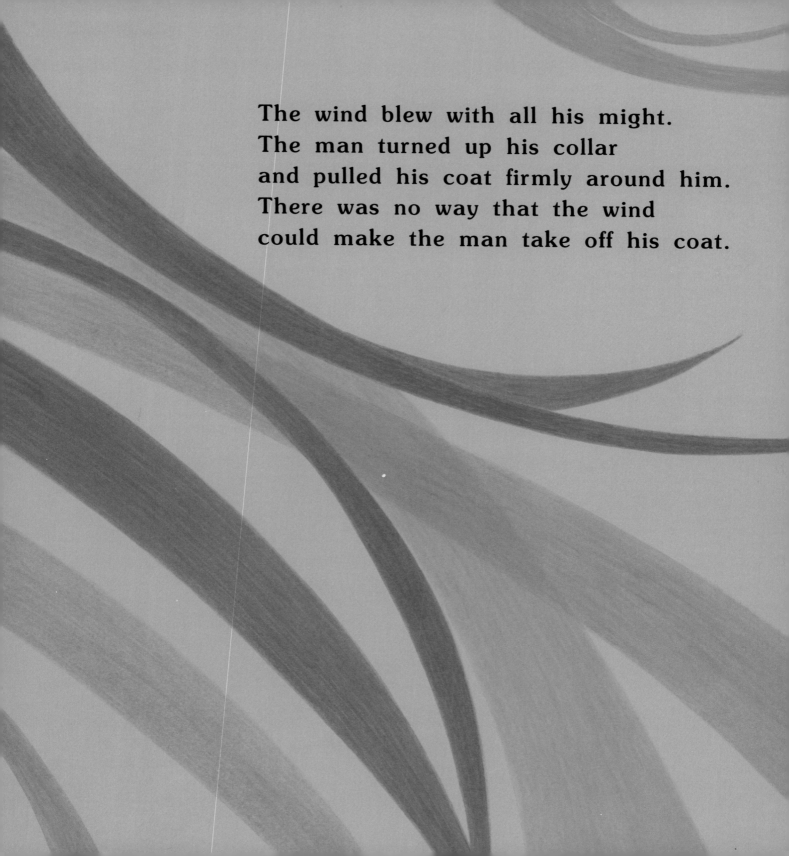

The wind blew with all his might.
The man turned up his collar
and pulled his coat firmly around him.
There was no way that the wind
could make the man take off his coat.

The sun laughed. "Give up?"

The wind was all out of breath.
"All right. You try it," he sighed.

The sun smiled warmly down on the man.
The man looked up at the sun
and unbuttoned one of the buttons on his coat.
The sun smiled still more warmly.
The man unbuttoned another button.

The sun smiled even more warmly.
The man unbuttoned the third button.
His coat was flapping open.

Now it was getting hot!
The man took off his coat,
hung it over his arm,
and continued on his journey.

"Which is stronger,
love or force?"
asked the sun.

The wind did not answer.
He slid into a hollow to rest.

The sun smiled warmly

and is still smiling today.